Poetry
Introduction 6

Poetry
Introduction 6

faber and faber
LONDON · BOSTON

First published in 1985
by Faber and Faber Limited
3 Queen Square London WC1N 3AU

Filmset by Wilmaset, Birkenhead
Printed in Great Britain by
Whitstable Litho Ltd, Whitstable, Kent
All rights reserved

British Library Cataloguing in Publication Data

Poetry introduction.—6
1. English poetry—20th century
821'.914'08   PR1225

ISBN 0-571-13543-9

CONTENTS

PUBLISHER'S NOTE

In the *Introduction* poetry anthologies we aim to publish poets whose work has hitherto been available only in magazines or booklets with a very limited circulation, thus giving them the opportunity of making their first appearance before the general public. The number of contributors is small, which means that we have been able to publish a representative selection of work from them all. Each of the eight poets in this volume has his or her own individual voice, but we feel that they all share consistent qualities of intelligence and perception.

This book has been published with financial assistance from the Arts Council of Great Britain.

SUSANNAH AMOORE

Long Sight

If I squint
I can nearly see myself now
As I was in that
Childhood-like summer of '71:

Recklessly freckled,
Sandals a tangled cat's cradle,
Whiskered straw hat
Shading sun-striped hair;
And wearing, I think,
A blurred Liberty print –
The dress smudged softly with
Clover pinks
And warm with the sun.

I blink, then a glimpse
Of the cat
Who twitchingly dreams life
Away on the lawn
Beside me, stretched flat
In the heat
Like tabby elastic.

Now I am focused and clearly smiling,
Lovingly stroking, no longer
Dimmed or distorted.
I must have been happy,
Though I can't quite
Catch my eye
To find out.

At the End of April

The sun still waits in the back of the sky,
But it's warmer now; great bunches of leaves
Come shouldering, clambering
Up through the earth, overnight it seems –
To be ready for poppies, perhaps,
Or stiff stalks of golden plate.

The birds, now perfectly certain,
Speed low over the Green, with beaks clamped tight
On difficult bits for nests;
While beneath their flight
The wicket is being carefully cut and measured
For an early game.

Old people emerge from winter to sit
Again round the edge of the Green;
And when they lean forward to talk,
Or throw bread to the birds, or sniff the twirling
Cuttings of grass, they lean away
From the lettering carved on the backs of their seats –

Words that say
Given in Memory of one who loved to sit
Here on the Green, and watch cricket –
Or the spring coming; or their time
Going; or whatever it was they
Saw in the afternoons.

Dawn in West Hampstead

I saw them once in an ordinary dawn
In a summer about ten years ago.
They swept past up the hill
In those moments when street lights fade
And before daylight gives back colours.
I remember the sharp night smell
Of the scented geranium,
Its unpruned arms spread around me
And sprawled through balcony railings.

There seemed to be dozens of them.
Soldiers, police? I couldn't tell,
It didn't matter. But not one
Of those riders looked up.
They were far too intent on the Heath.
And seen from down there on the horses
I'd be only a tired white glimmer
Of nightdress catching on rust
In the breeze, with a quietened baby
Slung on a shoulder in the way
That soothes. And they couldn't have seen
That my toes were cold
And curled over dead geranium leaves.

I never saw them again. They were
My secret, my magic. Once or twice
In the next couple of years
Clattering hooves like far-away thunder
Would wake me,
And I was happy to think of them
Racing the sun to the Heath
And kicking aside damp dandelion clocks.

About to be Happy

It was a cold dry spring,
With no consoling greening rain to feed
The divided border plants,
Or soften grass.

Noisily, the crows returned; and wrenched
At living twigs to build again their great black
Wiry cradles; and swayed sky-high
Above the park.

Now the nests are emptying;
Bulky young birds teetering on the edge of
Flight to that far sun-white cloud, that
Unfamiliar tree; while all around,
Blown seeds drift
On heated air.

A breeze stirs; leaves unfurl. Gently,
The year is rolling over into summer,
Smoothing the sharper edges of damaged days
It leaves behind.

Trees

Above all, I should find it hard
To abandon these trees,
This parkful of branches and leaves
That for years I have watched grow
Thicker, greener, closer —

So close now to these tall windows
That I think their green fingers
Reach out to the glass, claiming
This room, as if they finally
Belong inside.

Already they have forced me
To choose a particular pattern
Or colour or shape in here;
They are doubled in gilt-framed
Mirrors, matched in green carpet;
And on one wall there is a painting
Of trees: a picture strangely
Composed of all those colours
That are trapped and flickering
In my opal ring – pinks
And mauves and blues.

But the trees I speak of are
Green and only green to me;
And tonight, out there, beneath
The growing dark, they wait;
Enfolding their birds: having
Power, these trees,
Such power.

Poem for My Daughters

One summer soon,
If they are tired, as I am,
Of crowded easy heat and bright blue seas,
I shall take my daughters back
To Northumberland.

We shall return to the long pale beach
With the castle built on its rocks
That I loved when I was a child
With salt-thick hair.

Perhaps in a year or two we shall be there.
And then one day, on Bamburgh Beach,
If you should search in the mist
That presses on cheeks soft, cold, damp,
Like a fine white curtain,
You might see us.

Look for a mother with a child on each hand –
Girls with sharp little shoulders
And new front teeth too big for their faces,
The edges still frilled.
They will be there on the empty shore
Wandering along the line of the tide,
Suddenly stooping to examine a pebble
Or part of a shell, liking the feel
Of the cool shift of sand under their feet.
They will shout and point to a swimming dog
Or the red-legged gulls,
A puffin, a seal.

I wonder if you have seen us by now
As we brush the sand from our shells
And move on to the castle. The North Sea
Waits on the left, wickedly grey and cold,
Experienced at fingering wrecks,
Smoothing bones.
Have you heard the sound
Of the waves muffled in mist
As they bulge and burst on the beach?

On our right are dunes, the sand knitted
And spiky with the grass that cuts
And scattered now with white
Buttons of thrift.

And if we should meet at the castle
Will you say to yourself,
Ah yes, I see what she means, it is peace.
Or shall I see through the mist your face,
Uncomprehending?

Palace House Garden

When I look at the lawn
under the trees
in the garden next door,
unrolled last week
from a hundred strips or more
of grass, I see it lies
like an invalid, gathering
strength; and I am touched
by the sight of its
seams, its yellow state.

I know by the summer
the lawn will have grown,
and be cut into lengths
and shades of green,
but I think I shall miss

what used to be there –
that tangled mass of brambles
and nettles, foxgloves and roses
and weeds, all eager to keep
their tight, excited
grip on the garden.

An Upstairs Kitchen

It is strange that I used to think
The summers were best in this kitchen
High in the back of the house:
A time when thick greens
From the trees and the park beyond
Smother the windows
And enter the room.

A time when I easily leave the peeling
Or cleaning to drift and lean
On cool glass, drawn
By the astonishing pink of the jay,
By short bare legs which distantly
Lift the swings, by the dog
Racing the trains.

Strange, because now is clearly the time
I like best. The Bank Holiday fairs
Crammed close round the oaks
Have all gone; old ginger leaves
Are heaped soaking and deep in their place,
And the footballers' turkey-red shirts
Flare through the branches.

And some days, on the top edge of the far
Distance, through bare trees,
I can see the tower of the riverside
Church, where a mother lies
Buried with six of her children,
Three of them drowned
At different times.

How surprised she might be to know
That more than a century later
I worry in winters
Over her carelessness and pain,
While the iron gently noses its way
Between buttons and pleats
With soft steam sighs.

Late Afternoon in Autumn

Because of the wind and a darkened sky,
It is hard to distinguish which of the swirling
Things in the air are leaves;
Which are birds
Setting off.

Soon, steeped in the glow of the gold,
Greens and pinks of a room lamp-lit by tea time,
I shall barely remember those restless
Summer accomplices thrown
In a cupboard upstairs –
Thin cotton dresses; dangerous,
Bright-coloured sandals:
We all conspired
To feel free.

Now, half asleep by the fire, I watch
While the children, warm polished hair hooked
Behind ears, play their kind of patience;
I hear the soft, silk slap of cards
As they land; spades
On spades, hearts
Upon hearts.

SHIRLEY BELL

Work in Progress

'Good evening, ladies. As you know, this is a course of
ten lessons and we'll each complete a collage house.
This form lends itself to simplification – the broad,
applied shapes – and to endless decorative elaboration,
with stitchery, sequins, beads, et cetera.'

The guipure moon wears a strange face,
self-regarding, it shuts her out or in.
She is piecing a spread velvet sky
– like warm fingers in her hair, that gentle tug –
and stopping the blind windows
with a tissue of muslin sewn with bars.
How her fingers fly!

Tonight her baby's cry came with her,
such a fine needle. And now there is a woman
with a stitched white face, turning
from the dolly faces pressed against the glass.
Her scissors snap. Perhaps next week . . .
embroidered feet, running,
where moonshine stripes the street.

This needs some gathering of threads, a neatening.
Does she stay or go? But there's only an appliquéd house
with a woman at the threshold, bound, irresolute.
No prick-pin messages: just too many knotted ends to cut,
and a myriad little stitches which hem her in her place.

Strandline

The wind stalks the salt marsh.
Pale sedges bow and scrape to a fractured sky
which shivers in the water-stands.
The fluted dunes are seeded –
with rabbit droppings, thrush anvils;
small cemeteries of snails.

A redshank triple chinks its danger.
Her head is turning, but beside her he is still,
with an emptied face, blank as water.
Skylarks rise and fall, rise and fall –
she tells him, 'Those could be on wires.'
Her words are snatched away
and side by side they move like marionettes
where blackthorn roots clench the sand.

The landscape is encoded in an idiom of signs –
here an opened gull's egg, there one fraying wing,
beached in the stranded mermaids' purses.
The sea is just a smear. 'Do you recall . . . ?'
The memories shimmer briefly,
but beneath their feet the transient dunes
are sifting through the marram strands,
and they're wearing different faces now.

Stillbirth

Poor hollowhead,
I talk to you in your walnut sleep
but your face forgets to move:
in my arms I hold a stranger

with voracious eyes,
wound in your yellowed shawl.
Such a thin tissue
between sleep and waking,
presence and absence:
in dreams I presented you
to roomfuls of strangers.
Now I'm talking to you
but, bone-quiet, you do not answer.
Poor hollowhead,
this is your sister,
who sleeps less quietly,
and in your place.

Enamelled

The furnace opens on
              to one red eye
which does not blink.
              The salted copper is balletic
on its stilt and glides from
              blood through black to
white-hot shimmerstroke.
              Then mirror glass. Call
it marriage if you like.
              This enamelled blank is
burning on my palm,
       a t t e n u a t e d
              glass and copper, clutched
as tight as intercourse
              and
       as various. Yet only let it
                            fall.

27

A sudden shock
                will rive it through and through.
                Now it
  hangs
between my breasts from
                      slender fetters
   Eggshell brittle. Heavy
                  as loving.

The Still Room

All year the room grew drowsy
with slow mouth-music, breathing
through fermentation locks.

After the sunlight, the air
was iced beneath the trees.
Lace overflowed the trugs:
odd flat-faced elderflowers, then
their must, feline in the darkness.
Drugged bees of yeast rose until
the jars thickened to pale honey.

The year closed on button eyes,
glittering from the elderbranches;
the royal purple of their juices.
Then heartbeats, and the soft curd,
gathering like sleep. Slowly
shadow fingers bubbled into sight,
semaphoring through the glass.

It lies on its side now, that year,
siphoned and sealed in pied rows –
Tyrian and straw-gold brimming
with another spring, another autumn.
And out beyond these racks,
new seasons, splintered faces –
smashed glass, smashed glass.

The bottles chink together;
their throats are stopped
and growing tired of waiting.

Stock-Taking

Today, the sky is heaped above
a rudimentary smudge of puddled fens;
along the dyke, the water is ridged and olive.
The wind turns it over and over.
He is carrying his pain carefully – a reliquary,
or something brimming, which he must not spill.

The tractors are awash, axle-deep
in a green, school-knicker sea of brassicas
and, against the sky, the long-barrow clamps
are ossuaries for yellow mangolds.
Out on the chequerboard fields a straggle of sheep
mumble the sprout stalks, like obedient poodles.
Their bellies are lamb-fat.

All around him his farm is laid out,
a spreadsheet, an itinerary of routines.
Yet all he can see is the careful doctor,
pulling the screens around those textbook eyes,

and telling him in a prescriptive tone
of lambs that he'll not fatten,
of glistening king-cups
whose drowned heads he'll never see.

She Warms Her Legs

Red snails of roses
stitch the pillows. Wax seals.
In the dresser drawer
the letters are pale and crisp.
Yes, they whisper. Yes.
Her reflected face is folded
like the sheets her dry hands smooth.
Perfume bottles preen in shiny wood.
The air is lavender.

Downstairs. Safe kitchen smells,
her sifters side by side;
everything on time.
In the garden he is ticking
to a metronome of seasons.
His feet print the lino, his fingers
spill lettuce with clotted roots,
the piglet-pink radishes.
Together they mould intaglios of days
until tall strangers quietly
pull the front door shut and leave.
He follows –
to an uncertain destination.

Now seeds rattle in their packets.
The glasshouse door bangs to and fro,
then the mirrored garden shivers
and is gone. In the fragments
she has found a matchbox car;
her hands are tidying, tidying
the flaking paint . . .
Just for a moment,
she looks for a tousled boy.

The past is emblematic:
it smiles from the sideboard,
but her back is turned.
The gas fire hisses.
Passive in the wreckage,
she warms her legs.

The Mouths

The long sigh fogs the mirror,
and that big 'O' of sky
is gathered to the tunnel vision
of the contents of a blink.
The eelwet fens are filling.
The thick air drips where skittled trees
show their brown bones, their dark feet
in the litter of all that autumn coinage.

Only the grey road persists;
its sudden disclosures.
Ahead, behind,
the white mouth swallows it all:
the scaffolding of the tractor,
the clamps, the cauliflower sheep.

When the car stops
your veiled smile fills my window,
and a coat as grey as mist.
I know at once that I, too,
will button my fogs around me
and shut you out.

Ice-Fall

The chill mirror is a lens
focusing deceits and reversals.
The brush flickers and wet lips pout,
eyes are fringed, lace, black.
Fingers like Braille,
tasting the subtle dimpling of crêpe,
the icy slip of silk, of winter satin.
And coiled around the throat,
the string of frozen pearls:
fumbled, snapping.

'Are you there? I missed the bus . . .'

The lens shivers and stills.
Arrested in the mirror
his fractured image
and his shocked wife,
and in his ears
the steady drip of cultured pearls.

Glasshouse at the Botanical Gardens

In here it's tropical.
The birds darn the air
and hum in the steamy levels.
A fine needle of water
stitches the undergrowth
to an embroidered circle,
where goldfish nudge the bellies
of the knotted waterlilies,
and the white lips tremble.

The flowers are appliquéd:
Strelitzias knit their beaks together.
Bromeliads yawn with leathery mouths,
thick with spittle and dead flies,
and the orchids' throats are
clotted and cervical.

Boot-button eyes
glitter on the gravel:
the toy mouse trembles
with its mouth darned shut.
Where the blood thickens,
flies lay eggs in the teddy bear fur.

S.E.G. CURTIS

Too Bloody Nice

He was too bloody nice, oh too bloody nice,
Couldn't say no, and he paid the price,
Went out with Marie, who's as cold as ice.

She cooked his dinner, she tidied his flat,
And then she moved in, and that was that.
He paid the price, he was too bloody nice.

She booked a hotel, he didn't say no,
He got her a child, we told him so,
Ignored our advice, he was too bloody nice.

Gun-shot wedding, honeymoon in Greece,
Marie was as shrewd as a chief of police,
He was too bloody nice, what a sacrifice.

He was too bloody nice, just too bloody nice.

Roy and Linda

The renovated forge in which
    Roy and Linda live, in Wales,
Is fresh with stripped pine furniture
    Picked up at auction sales.

From Linda's hand-thrown grey-green mugs
    We sip our herbal tea;
The kitchen's spotless freezer purrs
    Most self-sufficiently.

By the Laura Ashley curtains
   There's an elegant chaise-longue.
'We found this old maid in Tregoyd:
   And she flogged it for a song!'

'Buy cheap, then scrape; clean up; resell
   Sideboards, dressers, wardrobes, chairs . . .'
(Deschool the kids, make love, not war,
   Damn the rat race, stocks and shares.)

'The Dutch are keen on chests, you know,
   With linenfold, and solid oak . . .'
'The Mitsubishi truck's just *great*;
   Aren't we glad we left the "smoke"?'

So natural to sit and share
   The 'lifestyle' Roy and Linda chose,
Decry the sins of capital
   Among the bibelots.

The Adrian Mitchell Kits

You buy them at the Do-It-Yourself,
   The Adrian Mitchell kits;
The masks are in polystyrene,
   Just choose the one that fits.

They aren't so cheap, I know, but then
   They're all Arts Council made;
The Extra has a lining of fur,
   The De Luxe is trimmed with suede.

But you can be a bohemian,
    A radical, one of the few,
In rubberized plastic, PVC,
    And as seen on telly, too.

Conjunctions

It's other stars you read out now, and not
My Capricorn and your Aquarius,
Whose conjunction under sunny Leo
That August glowed so bright for us.

When grey-skied Libra came, I surely missed
Some later horoscope I should beware –
About 'new plans', the 'future', 'former friends',
Of course, and 'romance in the air'.

If he is Pisces, Gemini or Cancer
I thank proverbial stars I cannot tell;
But wish all talk of seasons, signs and, yes,
Your new conjunction deep in hell.

Market Street

In a wash of autumn crowds, we stop to kiss goodbye;
    You've only just got time to buy some things for tea.
You're sorry, but there, you've a family to cook for;
        I'm so lucky, you add. I'm free.

We stop to kiss goodbye. Then I am free to go,
    With prospects wide as seas, yes, choice on every hand;
The town my oyster, each evening hour my own,
        And life my kingdom to command.

Dear, do you covet this, my range of liberty,
  Weighed down by shopping, in the store's slow queue?
Oh, if you just sensed how blank its compass seems,
    As I walk up Market Street, away from you.

Sports Extra

Supremos of the rugby song
And warm backslapping clannishness
Boom unmelodiously along
The emulsioned brick passages.

The smell of Algipan and mud
Wafts pungently in draughty air.
The hot-pot's brewing at the back,
The first pints clinking in the bar.

By biroed squash-court booking sheets
Hang *Ladies Night* and *Coaching Pool* . . .
'When Bev went through, that bleeding ref
Could least have played advantage rule!'

How Nobby came to slice his kick
We'll never know; nor how nor why
The Firsts went down, mid-week; nor how
Tom sold that dummy for his try . . .

Post-mortems on a thousand games
Flow rich as Boddingtons, or Bass.
Beyond pavilion bonhomie,
On dark, dank flats of deserted grass

January squalls of rain fling down.
Vans with Sports Pinks hiss through town.

August 1983

A red machine, bungalow-sized,
Eats endless acres, band by band;
This year's yield being maximized,
And not a soul. Just empty land.

Insistent as muzak, its motor
Whines through a doldrums of wheat:
No poppy, no heartsease, no tare.
Owner's a Board in Lombard Street.

Where fathers shared thanksgiving for
Bread once hallowed, and the earth's fruits,
We stand apart now, more and more
Estranged from what were common roots.

In evening classes we could learn
To fashion things like harvest bows:
Be told of scythe and stook and churn
And what pleaching was, I suppose.

Gathered here, once, in harvest week
Was fellowship – beyond recall.
Such fertile land, so lonely bleak,
Now quickens with no love at all.

Colleague

Our colleague, Ernest Old, expounds
    To first year 'kids' upon
Metadiegetic discourse
    In Dickens and in Donne.

He thinks he'll make a Chair before
  He's thirty-eight or so;
His latest work is due out soon
  On Methuen Video.

Archaic bourgeois structures must
  Dictate a bourgeois text:
That methodology once grasped,
  It's hermeneutics next.

He's a brand-new desk computer
  For poems he takes to bits.
'The author's dead', you understand;
  In his place our Ernest sits.

O Tempora . . .

The Poly Annexe – Arts canteen:
  Fluorescent tubes light bleakly up
Breeze-block wall, Ban Vivisection,
  Formica tables, cardboard cup.

Jack, with his dog-eared Foucault,
  And grey in moustache and hair,
Rolls a thin spike of Caporal,
  Eyeing with rue the students there.

Few takers, these days, for his course
  Called 'Post-War Bourgeois Structures One'.
Lynda, his wife, 's lost faith (and looks),
  Said last night *Wodehouse* was fun.

They don't make love much now and, Christ,
   The kids prefer Blackpool to France,
And raved the week she took them to
   That crappy *Pirates of Penzance*.

The Poly rugby team lolls where
   His Media Studies group once sat;
Critiques by Sartre, Lukács' Theory –
   Then they knew where it was at.

Those Woodstock years! Of Them and Us,
   Change dialectically explored,
While Lynda's nightschool Brecht helped pay
   For town house, Audi, vacs abroad.

Oh whither dreams of social science?
   Marcuse? Laing? (His pint is gall.)
And now there's cuts, and no one's safe . . .
   The rugby team starts 'Nobby 'All'.

ALAN DEWAR

Criggion

For my father

When the shocks have been set
he watches for the rock's
tension failing
like glaciers calving; listens
for the deep weight of surrender
as gravity delivers
usable rubble.
Stone of depth,
split from the dark cliff
when the charges and jackhammers bit,
thinned to a stone of the surface.
His own system moves in
in stages, rendering
the crag to grades.
The roads are the reason
but the quarry is the man loving
the moment of give.

Industry

1

Forget those time-softened mills,
forget the quiet renewals
spilling power through the race.
Ignore the sadness, entropy
of solar silence dimming
on our bright panels. Look:
sky is the black of absence.

The firth is like mercury.
Against the water, complex black
steels and concretes cluster.
Waste flares off, fierce worklight
is fired at the groundplan.
Roads bend in like lines of force;
are gridded into service,
spiralling round towers.
Matt blocks absorb
material, transform.
Kiln of the great anarchy.

2

Long sag of heavy wires drawn out of town,
empty road unrolled into the farmlands,
car stilled, fuel burned.
                    Stubble fires consume.
Red combs ripple over black earth burning
lines of the waste crop out of ground.
Carrion angels move through the last smoke
shading to no colour above the trees;
lift heavily like black flakes on updraft,
weighting their turns, stunned with the end of things.

3

When the blast has locked the quarry face
a man ropes down. He knocks
and levers, braced, balancing
across the faults. Still settling,
the valley closes in. He works
towards the keystone holding
fractures clenched.
Veins of air fasten unsound rock.
Found, he pauses. Gauges.
Wraps a loop around his thigh.

Now become part of the measure:
truth or failure.
He sets the bar. A glance,
then gives his own weight to the flaw.
Far inside the mass, the lode of air
registers, and the rock turns
on the pivots of its core and bursts.
In the sudden dance of moment
he must kick and ride
the tense pendulum
escaping the body
falling away, brief wraith
grounded on the rope's arc
returning as life gathers
to one completion of a ring of faith.

Canal

An area of breakdown:
but as the city falters, one simple
surface of resolved stress.

Frictionless, a long channel
like an ingot of water,
hung now with dead loads.

Trailing hawsers enter
bright meniscus circles
on the black level.

Deep hulls
make hollows
in the still enamel.

The water outlasts
recession of material:
abraded brick, tackle gone out of use.

In the clutter of failure,
such form is final.
This is the clean plane of function:

a blade concealed in the clothing.

Dawn Shift

It all makes sense: the markings on the floor
refer to grids on clipboards;

the loading dock is stacked in the order
of orders. The warehouse is quiet.

The stocked racks are unattended.
When the clatter starts, I'll start.

The voices come to man the aisles,
filling through the forklift passages.

The ghostly docklight fades out
past the shadow of the canopy,

past the long, swung perspectives where the artics wheel,
poised on the pads of their tyres,

past where I can see. It all makes sense.
Past it all is the sky's big indiscipline.

Free Enterprise

1

I'm waiting here, stocked up,
coping, where no one else
will want to come.

When they go gunning
for the well-managed farms,
for the secured complexes,

my woodsmoke, tarred roofs
scruffy among thistles
will be irrelevant.

The men first to the landrovers
will rule while the loot lasts,
while there are still old scores.

Then when the grids fail
and the rough grass breaks through,
I'll come out, fittest.

2

All right, so the nasal wind
makes your cavities ache
and changes the view
in spite of the marram.
So what if the sea gnaws?
The camp is sanitary,
double-glazing snug.
This isn't the hardest option:
the supplies are regular
and we know what can happen
from the mainland histories.

The dead singers keen
in our headphones;
our acceptance is verified
by their burn-outs:
we've done the right thing.

3

The city's designs are exposed:
perspectives open
as the fabrics decompose.
That howl is air
sounding in chambers.
The mute layer of crowd
has cleared like groundmist.
Broken vaults boom.
We keep away,
well out where there are just
the fast rows of posts,
the damage and the quiet
resonance of wires.

Jobs

I sit on, trying to think of something,
in spite of jobs ripening around me.
Light drives down, settles impeccably
in stiff volumes on the stone tiles,
until the plant she brought to convalesce
is loaded with light.

I'll study the flaring stems
holding the pale steady light
in liquid capillaries.
Instead of making a grab to the heart,
fixing it as a totem of something,
I'll leave it as a few minutes
participating, learning to husband.

Hangover

An attic room, untidy, distorted.
A wedge of light drops through the sloping wall.
A foot set on the floor, testing:
the houseframe holds.
The steady medium of air parts,
closes, admitting the careful limbs,
the vessel head.
           Eyes adjust,
scoping unfamiliar depths
from the bone orbits.
At the sink, the glancing
difficult light in the tap flow,
small distortions in the window blisters.
Across the yard, an asphalt skin
on pounded rubble, bolts
holding pipes, open treads
bitten into the brickwork, all
ache into sight.
On the sill, a plant burns like a message.

Basic Training

The victims are mustering.
In their grim barracks
all the leaned-on, hammered men
have mastered one-finger disablement.

The stared-at women work out all the time:
they gird their tits
and limber their pelvises
as if they were riding elephants.

The late developers
have forgotten the stunners who ditched them;
they jockey for precedence
in the chains of command.

When word comes through
to cut loose, these shock troops,
astonished, make their way
out across a world awaiting vengeance.

As it dawns, they weep with glee.
They nurse the delicate
triggers of their own wiring,
rigged, they're almost sure, to self-destruct.

Peak Cavern

On my first paid holiday
the job will not recede:
half-smiles and bargains follow
as I walk into the ground.

Water hollows, growing stone like fungus.
Sockets drain. My head stays full
with the forced light of rooms
and the guide's understatements:

'These natural caverns
are linked to the castle by shafts.
The Duke had no qualms: he dropped
power-seekers, miscreants.

'Stand still, I'll demonstrate
the last word in darkness.
Those who survived the fall
starved with their eyes struggling like this.'

Waiting here, hooded in black,
all the business of the surface
seeps away: the ploys of small control
are founded on this open dark.

There is only the distance of rock,
the flex of working water
deriving its own lines
inside the world.

Meditation Overcoming Desire

Although I know
the movement of the breast depends
on operation of internal sacs,
and the full voice on glossy diaphragms,
and the line of cheek and eye
on the smug truth of the skull set in us,
it doesn't help.

Curbar

For Ron Fawcett, seen soloing on Curbar Edge, Derbyshire, July 1980

The gritstone fault
brows the air to Cheshire.
Its harsh grain
quickens our fingers
so we feel like safecrackers.

The quartz pebbles
and the flared, awkward fissures
offer us pinchgrips and off-width jams –
bravado, technical talk,
the odd intensity.

Strapping in gear
we watched someone climb
on bonespan only, flesh tension:
the held water of a body
balanced in the huge

flux of rock and air.
The long slopes out of Bleaklow
broke suddenly above us,
their sharp grasses
scoring the grey light.

Below us in the crag rubble
rowan got started,
the pretty boundaries,
neat farms soon after.
Between waves of earth we watched.

When we know that every effort,
every moment taken for ourselves,
is cheated from our death
like a loophole
in the business of generations,

can we even want
to move as clean as that?
He swung gravity
through the fulcrum of himself,
saying we can.

Cotgrave

Spread on the mineshaft
like a heavy parasol,
a village with a town stuffed into it.

A sleight of land
keeps the place out of camera,
the bedded bricks multiplying like cells.

Easy enough
to take the cheese-scabbed grill
and balding towel as a handy text:

'To test the ultimate
performance of materials,
the stresses must be gauged at the exact

point of failure.'
Cotgrave: the name offers itself
as a paradigm of the reduced life.

Easy to accept
the insistence of the shut face;
everyone's privacy; everyone's blame.

The dogs go under
unseen obstacles. The place
is an installation of kept distance.

'Huge and Mighty Forms'

For James Dewar

We left the vehicles,
entered tree-slowed light,
kicking a mist off the grass,
moving like legends . . .

To him, the forest was a set
of signs of management:
hardcore gradients, blazed trunks,
truck-scored ruts.

Tree sequences frayed
to a litter of lumber:
the clearing opened out a lens of air
across the glen.

On the far slope, the treeline marked
striated light and stone
from a pad of dark green
shaved with fire breaks.

Further in, the tree-dark split
to the tall wound we'd come to see,
a limb of water, torn
into huge force by its dropping weight.

I nudge the place with blunt romance
of waterfall and mountain.
He works with design
and a system of blades.

Snooker
A commentary

Here in the plush light
it's all postures and frictions
as the top men
take each other on.
Soft chalk twists
on to the tips of cues.
A hard clack
as spin transfers
among crystallite balls,
and the angular force
spends itself cleanly
against hard
but resilient cushions.
He leans to snug
another red, like fate,
it seems, participant
in the absolute
planar connections
on this field of simplicity.

Now watch:
the champion's
stunning behind
the black; sustaining the break;
now screwing into baulk
for safety, certain of the frame.
This hushed cross-section
of the world's gravity
allows those of us
who sit in the watching darkness
to envy and love
these pure transactions,
as if such concentration
on the physics of perfect release
could, after all, annihilate.

STEPHEN KNIGHT

The Gift

My parcel was delivered to the college
Thoroughly packaged, like an only child . . .
I tear my father's beautifully written note
(*Please acknowledge receipt, Love Mum & Dad*)
Then fold the wrapping for possible re-use.
A breeze laps the posters crusting the wall;
Like lily pads, they compete to face the light.

I bump into Philip inside the Lodge.
He asks to see the gift – another four-sleeved
Pullover! Raising it shoulder-high, he
Teases me about the additional arms
Till I make my excuses and leave him
At the pigeonholes to scurry to my room.

I lay the jumper on my coverlet
And step back to survey the lively design –
Summery shades of green and blue in bars
A centimetre wide around the middle;
And seagulls, too. Trying it on before
My full-length mirror, I turn in circles like
A weather vane. The sleeves rotate with me!

Dizzier than Lewis Carroll's Alice, I
Finish instead an essay due at six . . .
My sides itch as I write. Just below the ribs,
Above my pelvis, carpal bones, knuckles,
And ten fingernails push through the flesh like roots.
Should I telephone home, or should I wait?

A Species of Idleness

The rise in temperature wakes me now . . .
The bedclothes gather at my ankles.
Dressing, I check if the street is wet
For the first time in weeks: our window-
box is spiriting away the dregs
From the teapot like a colander.
My bedroom is a pigsty. Last night,
I slept on the ceiling with the moths.

My parents have been anchoring me
To furniture since the Fifth of June –
I spend the afternoons sunbathing
With a weight on my feet. My head still
Rises up uncompromisingly.
The neighbours call me 'Dandelion' . . .
To cool myself, I lay my cheekbones
On our fat refrigerator door.

When a letter from Australia
Arrives, it's taken to the kitchen
Like a stack of dirty plates: I work
My way through the A4 sheets, clotted
With Tony's spidery hand. *Today,*
He writes, *I recorded the Outback –*
The clicking spokes of a bicycle,
The clack of hockey sticks from a field.

It's a bleak, vernal Sunday; the fish
In the river are counting their scales . . .
Your typewritten picture-postcards are
As cold as rubber gloves, and yet I
Stand them on my desk and mantelpiece.
Have you no time to send a letter?

Food is never off my mind. Weightless
And bored, I feed on every page's

Pieces of good advice: how to fill
The vacuum with games of patience
And botany – my hair is growing
Faster than the grass (so I settle
For dry shampoo) and the king of clubs
Reminds me of my two-faced father!
Despite my thorough shuffling, he
Continues floating to the surface.

Every breeze disturbs me. I flicker
With the leaves and the pages of my
Writing-pad like fire. Tending to drift,
I fill my pockets with stones and wear
A diver's metal boots, though they clash
With all my clothes. Tony recommends
Fresh air and plenty of fruit. My skin
Browns like bitten apple in the sun.

Theresa

Theresa let fall her copy of *Harpers & Queen*
   And as it struck the ground (among her clothes,
Books, and several pairs of fat, unfashionable shoes) be-
   came a bird: her long nose longer, her slim
Arms and fingers wings, and golden feathers everywhere.

Her father was dismayed, her mother quite reluctant
   To remove droppings from her cotton sheets.
They informed a priest: he took her silence to imply
   Apostasy – a thoughtless rebellion.
She sat plump in the middle of the bed. Would not budge.

The trendy priest assumed a pose of concentration –
  Skewering his clean-shaven chin with an
Oblong index finger. Then he blessed her, then he left.
  Mother makes Theresa shallow bowls of
Lemon tea. Bedside, Daddy delivers bulletins:

'I hang up when your spotty boyfriend telephones . . .'
  'Your mother is mixing gin and Librium . . .'
'I bought a new, smoke-blue Granada yesterday . . .'
  'Your mother insists on knowing when you fly . . .'
'The windows have been barred, we cannot let you fall . . .'

The Quiet Life

Fearing my reflection, I
Have banished mirrors from
Our room. 'Do you realize,'
She asks, 'that your face is
Wasting?' (Of course I do.) 'And
Look, abnormally white!'

We wall ourselves up with old
Encyclopaedias:
On ghosts, one entry insists
An explanation must
Be sought in the frame of mind
Of the person haunted.

Suspicious of the other
Tenants, we cook and eat
At midnight. Now and then, I
Venture to the bathroom
And watch a love-bite move through
Mauve to saffron on my

Throat, or comb my spiky shoots
Of unwashed hair. Every
Night, we listen for the sound
Of footsteps in the snow
And on the landing carpet –
Her bloodless, pretty face

Presses to our window like
The moon. Books lie open
On the floor: she steps from Kyd
To Swift as though they were
Floes of ice. We have begun
To stack them in the drawers

But still more drift to every
Corner of the room. At
Dawn, we slide into bed like
A couple of bookmarks.
Being cold, I gravitate
Towards her in the dark.

Dinner Time

'Her ten fingers' nine nails were pointed
And painted a leathery red,' she
Says without batting an eyelid, then
Hands me her grandmother's photograph.

'Her room was crawling with cobwebs; stale,
Diaphanous curtains; and fifteen
Christs on fifteen crosses – which always
Put me in mind of a rugby team.

'I once stayed all night by her smelly
Sickbed.' Lowering her voice, she walks
Her fingers along the tablecloth
To a fork – 'And cut her with a knife.

'A cut so big,' she says then, like an
Angler, holds her insubstantial hands
Apart. 'Well, she bled pure paraffin.'

Pure paraffin! So a haemorrhage
(I ask her) would amount to arson?
She offers me a flickering smile.

The Vivisectionists

Across the lawn his English neighbour
Stretches for the zip along her spine:
A clumsy action pushing out the breasts –
'Clumsy, but I like her pointed breasts.'

She wriggles out of her lemon dress,
Uncaps a tube of viscous tanning cream
Then smooths her warm and auburn body
Like a fly polishing six legs clean.

He lives below her room. On Saturdays
She relaxes with her stereo:
Prélude à 'L'Après-midi d'un faune'
Floats from her open window like smoke;

He brings up to date his diary's
Entries on the colour of her skin . . .
Last night, he wrote, 'A noise on the tiles
Outside. She's walking down the wall to me.'

Anatomy Class

Like a shiny pendulum, my brother returned home
At regular intervals. One afternoon in May,
He visited with a skeleton; I hadn't seen
His pink face pinker with enthusiasm since he
    Pushed a syringe in our mother's upper arm.

The bones were neatly stacked, like cutlery. 'Uterus,'
He murmured, 'liver, kidneys, bladder. . . ,' itemizing
Absent organs. Our parents – smiling at the mention
    Of every piece – continued with the dinner.

I picked my way through the vertebrae, the yellowing
Rib cage, and the jewellery of her misplaceable
Finger bones; our dining-room window faces westward
    And the sunset lit my brother's spectacles.

The skull would make (I remember thinking) a perfect
Paper-weight, despite the swastika scratched on the lid.
As we moved to the living-room for tea and éclairs
My brother packed the set of bones away. Sulkily, I
    Ran my finger down the spindly table's leg.

The Awkward Age

His diary is packed with non-events –
Like March the First *I got up late* and March the Third
My teeth are visibly longer, both my cheeks are furred.
When the eristic charm of female scents

69

Leads me on, I follow it till I'm heard.
He sniffs at the Rive Gauche in my room! – If I say
Anything at all to him, he either turns away
    Or stares at me with his big eyes. He purred

    Like a car in his bedroom yesterday,
Watching television with the curtains drawn. *Hair*
Sprouts like hair but quicker. Skin thickens. Claws grow out
                                 where
    Nails were bitten down – I'm quoting from May

    The Fourth. He is obsessed with girls: their hair,
Their hands, the colour of their eyes . . . *T. said hullo*
Again today – she even smiled! But she wouldn't go
    To the cinema with me. C'est la guerre!

    He's full of Wordsworth's poetry: like snow.
Books gather at the foot of his bed. When I tell
Him to tidy his things away, he says he's unwell
    Or working – he walks to the beach below

    The golf links almost every night! The smell
Of salt lingers on his trousers and his best tweed
Jacket for days. There's no need to go, I say, no need.
    (We can't seem to bring him out of his shell.)

    I love, he says on June the Tenth, *to feed*
The seagulls till they're nice & fat. They don't take fright
If I look them in the eye. Should I be less polite
    & try this trick with girls? Would I succeed?

Frosty looks are bad enough, but he might
Stop walking with a stoop for me. *Why can't I be*
(He writes on June the Twenty-Third) *smooth-skinned &*
sexy?
We get no peace. He shaves three times a night.

The Diving Board

As Achilles lolls beside the pool
In dappled Bermuda shorts, he sips
Gin and orange juice from a tumbler
And strums the water's tuneless surface
With a pilose, tanned paw. Fish gather.

His white, athletic wife is bouncing
On the diving board. Two face-lifts old,
Her skin is stretched like canvas across
A frame of unexceptional bone:
A picture of health by Picasso.

His stationary manner annoys her,
She hectors him and keeps herself trim
With aerobics. Achilles has laced
The deep end with barracuda, he
Believes in living dangerously.

SARAH LAWSON

Cabo de Palos

Rollers come in like the wake
Of ships beyond the horizon
Out of sight under the blue edge
As I sit eating orange sections
On the balcony, January or not.
We mopped the tile floor yesterday –
Wet, it went porphyry-red;
It dried in shapes
Where the sunlight landed.

The offshore rocks balance on white saucers,
Some days nearly dinner plates.
The waves claim attention
Like the flames of a bonfire,
No two quite the same.
I watch them like a child
Eating popcorn at the movies,
A pile of orange peels on the plate beside me.
Progressing landward like the still but moving
Lightbulb news, these low-stepped terraces
Of bluegrass show last-minute white.

Always later, indoors from the wind,
I see across the glass-doored wall
The dark blue dado of the sea.
Late at night the sound keeps on,
And, inland bred, I think it's vaguely wasteful
And ought to be turned off.

We Are a Committee of Two

We are a committee of two
Formed to deal
With your concerns, my concerns.
Take some misfortune, say:
One of us is a kind of plaintiff
And the other a kind of Samurai,
Outraged and waving weapons,
Furious as a train with failing brakes.
So misfortunes,
What we used to call misfortunes,
Are little shrinking things
Whispering, I didn't mean it, honest.

Spring in Friesland

You give me your memories
In the ribbons and wrappings
Of a birthday-festive farmhouse.
I walk through your youth,
Admiring everything,
Like a visitor on a day
When the public's not admitted.

The tulips on the windowsill
Bend graceful goosenecks toward us,
Straining to hear
What makes us laugh together so.

76

Any Hourglass Holds Just So Much Sand

I have seen my future in her whitened hand;
My warm blood will cool, as hers has now
(Any hourglass holds just so much sand).

Unexpected scissors snip the magic band –
The woodsman's axe splits off the crucial bough –
I have seen my future in her whitened hand.

We trespass on a borrowed land,
Leave obscure paths through forest, bog and slough
(Any hourglass holds just so much sand).

My moving, muscled arm is live and tanned,
But life, it lasts a moment – I think how
I have seen my future in her whitened hand.

A tree once felled can never after stand;
Every living thing at last must bow
(Any hourglass holds just so much sand).

Death marks its property with its pale brand,
The waxen page stretched smooth across the brow.
I have seen my future in her whitened hand
(Any hourglass holds just so much sand).

Newspaper Vans

In that hotel across the narrow foreign street
From the offices of the *Diario de Notícias*
She died, and all the time she tried to breathe
And we comforted each other
Delivery vans were loading morning papers.

77

I opened the window to give her air
Her frothy lungs could not hold
And the busy noise rose up those pre-dawn cliffs.

The biggest news on earth
Is that my mother is about to die,
But it doesn't figure in even small headlines
In the *Diario de Notícias* across the street,
Where the vans clatter like dustbin morning.

She lies on the bed trying to breathe
(Beside her the telephone I use,
Controlling my voice
Because I am saying lines in a play, surely),
And the shivaree
At the bottom of the ravine sees her out.
Does she notice the noise
Or only worry at the air,
Wanting to breathe it, noise and all?
In another half hour I am running
Through the lobby
With the ambulance crew;
The street is hotel quiet
Until our useless siren starts.
The paper vans have left;
The news is on its way to foreign breakfasts,
Except the real news.

Casualty Unit, São José

I sprint after them; I surprise myself;
All the adrenalin has gone to my legs.
I would race them anywhere –
With her body on their stretcher.
The young houseman on the graveyard watch
Glances me the truth, but
He proffers a carotid his thick coin
To bribe life back –
Nothing, even magnified.
He relaxes the earphones
To a trick necklace,
Not even bothering to shrug.
The nurse pulls up the blanket
Like someone switching off the picture
Before the story's over.
Indignant, I tug it down again,
Pettily bold, death my ally in defiance.

On the Beach

On the beach all the shells
Hoard up tales of waves
To confide to the first
Human ear that wants to know.
We scuff over them in boots,
Ignoring the high-fidelity gossip
Underfoot, intent on our own sound swapping.
Not quite agreeing, we define and trade,
Refine, accept, insist, sinking our thick treads
Rhythmically into the shifting shingle,
Carelessing bits of bivalve and fisted shells
Bursting to tell us all they've learned.

Going Up in the Eiffel Tower

Steel basketwork, like a cane seat
In three (at least) dimensions,
The Eiffel Tower is an old *clochard*
With a hollow leg
Where it stashes a little lift.

The cliché of it conceals
The wonder until the last minute
When the postcards fall away
And Monsieur Eiffel unveils his great design
Exerting no more square pressure on the earth
Than Monsieur Eiffel himself
Seated in a Second Empire chair.

On the way up to a still, stilted
Airplane meal in the tethered fuselage
We watch the Champ de Mars greenly sink
And Paris pop up like cardboard
In circle after circle of substitute horizons,
As though our motion upward
Makes ripples in the very Paris streets.

My Father on Monument Circle

My father is a rumour who has reached
My ears, a little list of attributes
Who played clarinet and tennis,
Won a prize in Tort,
And in the afterglow of Lindbergh
Went aloft in jodhpurs.

One warm day in 1935
Somebody snapped me a rare souvenir,
Stopped him in mid-stride
In a linen suit, developed him into an image
Before I had one. My father strides stylishly
In a wide pale hat, still in his twenties
Where it is always a summer before the war.
Later he tossed me half a baton
And then lost interest in the race.
I watch him now when he never guessed
I might be looking, thanks to the man
Who did me a favour for a dime one pastel summer.

R.A. MAITRE

Spelling It Out

Jain dusent ware enny.
What credence could we give
to such a two-a-penny

scrawl? And who wrote it?
It looked like the hand
that chalked, *I suked Jens tits.*

Did someone have inside knowledge?
And did this learning
take place under the bridge

where we ogled
such titbits of urban pornography?
The orthography

left much to be desired,
the content even more.
But what most fired

us was neither former nor latter
but last in this illiterate triad:
I dun Jan wit a frennsh leter.

Mimesis

...all poetry, from Homer onwards, consists in representing a semblance of its subject ... with no grasp of the reality.

Plato, *Republic*, Bk X

Stuck out in the rain,
the Bond girl in the bikini gets wet.
But it is only illusion:
her tiny billboard patio

is a desert island bliss
where cornflower skies
and a tangerine sun are eternal.
It is where heaven is.

The TWA jet next to her
is stuck in mid-flight.
It will never make it.

But, then, she is out of this world
and it but a sham Jumbo.
Q.E.D.

Hers is a tingling-fresh toothpaste smile,
for ever like the Mona Lisa's.

She looks the image of happiness.
Could you believe how flat she finds life is?

The Woman Underneath

On reflection, it all came down to nylon –
stockings, bras, pants.
Of course, there were the other things –
swing of buttocks, flap of breasts,

a whole shape of arc and indent.
But, somehow, it was the synthetics,
hitched nylon, an erotic mechanics,
that set us light years apart.

What did we have when we undressed?
Socks. Jockeys. A string vest.
But when they stepped out
of shoes, blouse, and skirt –

voilà! the French maid: that circumflex
of taut stocking-band; knickers
sheeny as courtesan's; the stripper's

unhooking acrobatics; and the Lautrec
girl stooping as puckered hose slithers.
They held us in a man-made scissors.

Intermezzo

The sun has gone west, and the moon
temps – orange balloon
sailing in over the trees.
Up the potato lines, hares

sprint before invisible greyhounds.
In the shelter of the coppice,
muntjaks nibble the ground –
bolt as they see us,

racehorse off across wheat fields
grown grey; silvering where
a few lights blink at us, the church tower's
broad shoulders hump the moon's gold.

Elevation

Mists lift; and a distance
is sketchily reinstated:
the powder-blue church where

dove-grey pigeons congregate;
puffs of incense-burning woods;
pale seas of wheat; pylons,

small in the valley, in silver
file like pilgrims from *Tannhäuser*;
the sun's raised monstrance.

War Games

It comes back: convoys
of army lorries, pondweed green,
soprano engines

damped in a mist across the commons
they vanished into . . .
A khaki girder bridge

we clanked across on sorties . . .
Paras' red berets,
the blacks of the Engineers –

like counters in backgammon . . .
Muffled booms . . .
Caterpillar tracks printed on the tarmac . . .

Muddy tanks
like hippos douching in a water bath . . .
Bagshot-sand rises . . . A silt path

angled like a rifle sight,
pointed at brackened spurs –
sudden clatterings, mews:

live rounds from the ranges,
ricochets' top Cs . . .
The toothy whistling of the breeze

as we clambered up a flinty hillside,
conquered the ridge where a red flag flapped
as though anticipating us . . .

Like lookouts, we'd spot
steam trains' telltale miniatures of clouds,
Dinky Toy transport betraying the roads,

the sea of sand we'd just crossed,
orange stretch, a few vague sheds
of corrugated iron,

gelatinous in a heat haze:
microcosmic theatre of war
where the railing of a Bren-gun carrier,

stuck on a slope like Sisyphus,
drifted out to us –
whine, whine, all afternoon.

A Midsummer Day's Dream

June burns and the sun stops dead; the sky
is all cornflower, whipped clouds
like soft ice creams; and the fields
are badged with poppies.

High in the Downs, you nod as
dipterans gyrate, spectral tractors drone,
swallows sickle thermals –
oneiric afternoon

when clouds are sculpted while you wait:
there St George's dragon,
here, a lion couchant;
when you dream of the glass blower in Brighton,

his hot dogs, his melting Bambis,
he exhales before your eyes,
down there where the sea sparkles
and sails make Euclidean triangles;

where the girls make vases in swimsuits,
or turn tobacco all over
on the strip of beach by the Marina,
all rhythm and blue yachts;

90

where old men, late editions under their arms,
ogle bulbous nubility,
the matter of page 3 dreams,
the stuff of virility,

the girls who show it all
to the cocky male with the beach ball;
where the sun burns – stops dead
on Midsummer's Day when nudists go to bed

as the sun rides the sea yet again,
seduced by gold silk sheets;
couples pet to strains
of schmaltzy music in ballrooms of romance;

saxophones mask the creak of the pier;
the old men consult tide tables;
the freewheeling cosmic cycles
lap up the years.

Bats in the Sunshine

. . . our minds . . . as Aristotle notes, *blink at the most evident things like bats in the sunshine.*

Aquinas, *Summa Theologiae*

A single wooden note,
then a score, mechanical
like slow-spun football rattles,
alert us to the cricket,

napping in wasp-stripe deck chairs
within the garden's boundaries –
and into our reveries
come the hook of bat, arc of ball, pairs

of hands in semi-articulate clapping,
as the pitches of willow on leather,
percussive flesh and bone, scatter
husks of sound in our direction,

out across ochroid fields
stubbly like the unshaven on Sunday.
Bowled out of our dreams but still dozy,
we blink like bats in the sunshine, the golds

and yellow-greens of a slumbering August,
the sun still bright as a new ball,
dazzling. Distantly, slow bells
from the church signal six. We rest,

an evening promised of slow sauntering
through the village, past the green
where still the linen men lean
into their game and the girls, aspiring

to marriage, fling freckled arms
about a victor. And
later, parting sounds,
motors revving, lilting voices, dim

chromes still painting the sky,
the wicket silent but for the high notes
of the homonymous bats
sounding out their introverted commentaries.

The Volunteer*

Suspended from normal duties,
he brings his past with him
like a picture in a frame –

those clifftop vigils,
those vivid skies
matched to his blood-red uniform.

Called to higher things,
he mounts guard outside a pub,
an ensign on an inn sign,

dark eyes on upstairs window panes.
Perhaps a girl taunts or snubs
him as she disrobes,

for his steady gaze
is not without bitterness,
and his bayonet stands to attention.

Who knows? It's all left hanging
as he stands in his square, sometimes swaying,
always legless.

*The Volunteer Inn, Lyme Regis

BERNARD O'DONOGHUE

Vanellus, Vanellus

When I'd forgotten them, you told me how
I saw them every schoolbound, misty morning,
Tattering down the sallow sky of winter.
Now I know them well: I see them every mile
By flocks and companies in roadside fields
As I drive onwards through these snowcast days
To sit at your bed evoking them for you.

O'Regan the Amateur Anatomist

The gander clapped out its flat despair
While O'Regan sawed at its legs with his penknife.
He looked at me with a friendly smile as blood
Dripped in huge, dark drips. I didn't protest
Or flail out at him, but smiled in return,
Knowing what grown-ups do, whatever breeds
About their hearts, is always for the best.
Worms are cold-blooded; babies learn in the night
By being left to cry. Another time (a man
So generous, they said, he'd give you the sweet
From his mouth) he halved a robin with that knife.
Finally, racing his brother back from a funeral
Down a darkening road he drove his car
Under a lightless lorry, cutting his head off.
I wonder what he thought he was up to then?

97

A Noted Judge of Horses

The ache in his right arm worsening
Morning by morning asks for caution.
He knows its boding, cannot be wrong
About this. Yet he is more concerned
For the planks in the float that need
Woodworm treatment before drawing in
The hay, and whether the coarse meadow
Must be limed before it will crop again.

Still in the pallid dawn he dresses
In the clothes she laid out last night,
Washes in cold water and sets off,
Standing in the trailer with his eyes set
On the Shrove Fair. As long as his arm
Can lift a stick to lay in judgement
Down the shuddering line of a horse's back,
He'll take his chance, ignoring his dream
That before September's fair he'll be mumbling
From a hospital bed, pleading with nurses
To loose the pony tied by the western gate.

Nel Mezzo del Cammin

No more overcoats; maybe another suit,
A comb or two, and that's my lot.
So the odd poem (two in a good year)
Won't do to make the kind of edifice
I'd hoped to leave. Flush out the fantasy:
The mid-point being passed, the pattern's clear.
This road I had taken for a good byway
Is the main thoroughfare; and even that
Now seems too costly to maintain.

Too many holes to fill, not enough time
To start again. 'I wasn't ready. The sun
Was in my eyes.' A goodbye way indeed.
Soon we'll be counting razorblades and pencils.

The Nuthatch

I couldn't fathom why, one leafless
Cloudcast morning, he appeared to me,
Taking time off from his rind-research
To spread his chestnut throat and sing
Outside my window. His woodwind
Stammering exalted every workday
For weeks after. Only once more
I saw him, quite by chance, among
The crowding leaves. He didn't lift
His head as he pored over his wood-text.
Ashamed of the binocular intrusion,
Like breath on eggs or love pressed too far,
I'm trying to pretend I never saw him.

Pompeiana

Scratching away for shards of singed, green tile,
They'll be trying to assemble Sunday mornings
From our pre-atomic age. Infinitely
Careful, they'll fit them all together
To display medals and competition shields,
Serenaded by their much-loved pumproom trio,
And sell postcards of unoccupied bikinis.

Will they be able also to decode
The stern prohibition on petting and horseplay,
Or to account for that funny, male strutting
At large through the changing-rooms? To rebuild
That miserable, suggestive, chlorinated ache
From girls trailing toes in the blue water?

Lane the Bonesetter

Proverbial wisdom kept us off the streets
And that's a fact. The art of talk is dead.
When we had shaken all our heads enough
At people's knowing in the olden days
(When a cow died they thanked Almighty God
It wasn't one of them), we'd contemplate
Our local marvel-workers. On the flat
Of his back for three years and more, surgeons
Could do nothing: Lane had him walking
The four miles to Mass inside an hour.

Incurably rheumatical myself,
I made him out at home above Rockchapel
Where the swallows purred approving in the eaves.
Bent at a crystal mirror, he was bathing
A red eye. 'I'm praying I won't go blind
From it. Do you know anything about eyes?'
Beyond having heard it said that his descried
The future, I did not. He rolled his sleeves
Back to his shoulder like a red-gloveless
Inseminator and got down to it.
I'm much relieved and think there's something in it.

Timing the Pigs

Having cautiously observed the fifties boom in them
We finally went into pigs, immediately before
The bottom fell out of the market.
'We never had any luck,' we said. 'We couldn't
Allow for the element of chance. The theory
Was fine. That's the way with the world.'

When the Beatles were big in 'sixty-three
I was listening to Rachmaninov Two in the quiet evenings.
No sex. But I knew I was right.
In nineteen-seventy-three, though, I bought *Abbey Road*
At an inflated price. There was more than you'd think to it,
Looked at from a strictly musical angle.

And in 'eighty-three I'm working for the Labour Party
During the Tory landslide. It's not the economy
That ought to be worrying us.
Wrong again, of course. But there is this long shadow
Over the world. I hope I'm wrong, but I can't help thinking
About the law of averages. I hope I am wrong.

But nobody's wrong all the time.
Or are they?

Beware the Crab

As soon as the all-hope-ending word is out
We start to shun them, writing them off,
Not safe until the orange earth's aspersions
Have drummed with the holy water on their parcels
Sealing them. And all our duty ended.

Back we turn to our own, composing lines
Of well-weighed sympathy to heal with tears.
Placebos can cure us; they're happy now.

Once I stood on a thrush with a broken wing
And, when it shrilled, I stamped it into peace.

They are a race more foreign than the Soviets;
Extremists, terrorists, beyond the fringe of lunacy.

Nominations Are Invited

There are people around so blind they couldn't tell
Przewalski's horse from Willie Casey's jennet.
Though Dominic's next to us had guinea-hens
Calling, 'Two clock! Two clock!' and a mauve turkey
Whose nose ran red skin continuously,
Our local book of field birds was transcribed
In a broad script: crow, duck or sparrow.
Poor inheritors of the gift of Adam.

On the way into the zoo, you'd never seek
The route shown in the map, but use directions
From somebody whose cousin went there once
Years ago. Emerging through the entrance,
You couldn't put a name to any species.

Yet still there lingered on behind your eye
Something the past or present left around
The place. Big cats in snow: a curiosity
There for you. Or some bird's dart of colour
Recalling fairy thimbles or dead man's fingers,
Purple and orange and hung with cuckoo-spit.

Father Christmas

It was May or June when I first glimpsed him
Not far away: at any rate, as ever, out of season.
Either when the twilight thrush proclaims
Unending summer, or when the guilty children
Rummage through dark wardrobes for Christmas parcels,
In he blunders with his awful timing.
Red suit pulled over his dustcoat any old how,
Beard hooked crooked from his ears, and thrusting out
His dread portfolio of unnaturalized Greek terms:
Aorta; cardiac; thrombosis. Or policeman's words
That make it all sound warranted:
Stroke; violent; massive; laboured; and arrest.

BIOGRAPHICAL NOTES

SUSANNAH AMOORE. Born in Shandon, Dunbarton-shire in 1941, and educated mainly at the Newcastle upon Tyne Church High School. She then worked for BBC Television in London. She lives in Richmond with her two daughters, and now works for the *Financial Times*. Her poems have appeared in the *New Review*, *The Times Literary Supplement*, a Poetry Book Society Christ-mas supplement and the *London Review of Books*.

SHIRLEY BELL. Born in Birmingham in 1950 and is now living on a Lincolnshire cactus farm with her physicist husband. She has a daughter, two small sons, and an Open University First in English/Art History. Her poems have been accepted for *New Poetry 8* and numerous magazines, including *Argo*, *Other Poetry* and *Giant Steps*, and 'The Still Room' was broadcast by the BBC in *Poetry Now*. In September 1985 some of her work will be appearing in a Rivelin Press anthology to be edited by Ian McMillan. She has just completed a collec-tion of poems and is currently working on her first novel.

S.E.G. CURTIS. Born in 1943. After a Burnley child-hood, Simon Curtis grew up in south Northampton-shire. He now teaches at the University of Manchester and lives in Stockport.

ALAN DEWAR. Born in Hamburg in 1953 and brought up in a series of army camps in Britain and Canada. He read English at the University of Nottingham and is now a teacher. A pamphlet of his poetry, *Geometry*, was published by the Danby Press in 1983; poems have appeared in the *New Statesman*, *The Times Literary Supplement*, the *Honest Ulsterman*, *Poetry Review*, *Encounter*, *Quarto*, *New Poetry 8* and have been broadcast by the BBC in *Poetry Now*. He was a prizewinner in the National Poetry Competition in 1982, and his poems appeared in the National Poetry Competition anthology, 1983, and Sotheby's Poetry Competition anthology, 1982.

STEPHEN KNIGHT. Born in 1960 in Swansea, he read English at Jesus College, Oxford. He is currently Writer in Residence for West Glamorgan Education Authority, having previously directed plays and worked with the handicapped as part of a community theatre project. He was a winner of the BBC Radio Wales New Plays Competition in 1984. His poems have appeared in the *New Statesman*, the *London Review of Books*, *Poetry Review*, the *London Magazine*, the *Literary Review*, *New Poetry 9* (Arts Council) and *Straight Lines*. 'The Awkward Age' was a runner-up in the 1984 National Poetry Competition.

SARAH LAWSON. Born in 1943 in Indianapolis and educated at the universities of Indiana and Glasgow. Her recent translation of *The Treasure of the City of Ladies* from the medieval French of Christine de Pisan for Penguin Classics is the first translation of the work in English. Her poems have been published widely in little magazines, and she reviews books for the *New Statesman* and the *Freethinker*. She has lived in London since 1969.

R.A. MAITRE. Born of a French father and an English mother in 1944 in Fleet, Hampshire, and educated at Farnborough Grammar School, Enfield College and

Bedford College, University of London. Until 1984 he was Senior Lecturer in Philosophy at the Middlesex Polytechnic, specializing in Aesthetics. He is now a freelance writer and translator. He was one of the first prize-winners in the 1982 *Sunday Times* Clerihew competition and six of his clerihews appear in *Other People's Clerihews* edited by Gavin Ewart (OUP, 1983). He also won prizes in the 1982 National Poetry Competition, and the 1984 Greenwich Festival Poetry Competition. His poems have appeared/are to appear in: *Poetry Review*, *Outposts*, the *Countryman*, *Country Life* and *Other Poetry*. He lives with his wife, a philosopher and writer, and his stepson in a small village in north Hertfordshire.

BERNARD O'DONOGHUE. Born in 1945 in Cullen, Co. Cork, where he still lives for part of the year. Educated in Millstreet, Manchester, and Lincoln College, Oxford, he teaches English at Magdalen College, Oxford. He has published books on medieval literature, as well as poems in a Sycamore Press pamphlet, *Razorblades and Pencils*, in *Poetry Review*, *Argo*, the *Honest Ulsterman*, *Buckle*, *Verse*, *Oxford Poetry* and *Poetry Ireland Review*. He has had short stories published in the *Irish Press* and elsewhere.